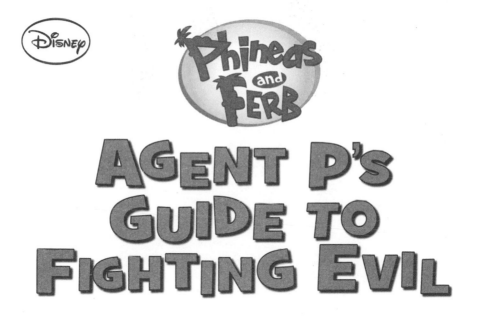

AGENT P'S GUIDE TO FIGHTING EVIL

By Scott Peterson

Based on the series created by Dan Povenmire and Jeff "Swampy" Marsh

DISNEY PRESS
New York

"Perry vs Doof and Doof and Doof" comic insert—Writer: Scott Peterson, Pencils & Inks: Scott Neely, Colors: Garry Black, Letters: Michael Stewart

"Baby Platypus" comic insert—Writer: Scott Peterson, Pencils: Min Sung Ku, Inks: Mike DeCarlo, Colors: Emily Kanalz, Letters: Michael Stewart

"Baby Trouble" comic insert—Writer: Scott Peterson, Pencils & Inks: Eric Jones, Colors: Garry Black, Letters: Michael Stewart

"Perry's Urgent Mission" comic insert—Writer: Scott Peterson, Pencils & Inks: Eric Jones, Colors: Garry Black, Letters: Michael Stewart

"Secrets from O.W.C.A." comic insert—Writer: Scott Peterson, Pencils & Inks: Eric Jones, Colors: John Green, Letters: Michael Stewart

Printed in the United States of America
First Edition
10 9 8 7 6 5 4 3 2 1
G475-5664-5-12306
ISBN 978-1-4231-6764-8
Library of Congress Control Number: 2012934136

For more Disney Press fun, visit www.disneybooks.com
Visit DisneyChannel.com

SUSTAINABLE FORESTRY INITIATIVE   Certified Sourcing   www.sfiprogram.org   SFI-00993

THIS LABEL APPLIES TO TEXT STOCK

TABLE OF CONTENTS

THIS IS IT. THE *REAL* TABLE OF CONTENTS. NO REASON TO LOOK ANY FURTHER.

SECRET TABLE OF CONTENTS

FOREWORD

So You Want to Fight Evil

Good afternoon! It's me, Carl Karl. I'm an (unpaid) intern for Major Monogram at the O.W.C.A. (Organization Without a Cool Acronym). We work with Agent P and dozens of other animal agents to fight evil every day. And since you picked up this book, it's pretty clear you want to do your part to stamp out evil as well. Well, you definitely came to the right place!

In this book you'll find vital agent information, top secret "how to's," and challenging training activities to test your creative abilities and hone your reflexes until you are (almost) as quick-thinking as Agent P. You will also discover agency jokes and comics (my idea!) . . . because even the highest caliber agent needs a little rest and relaxation to keep his or her mind at peak performance.

So find someplace private, make sure no one is looking, and turn the page.

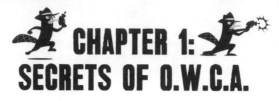

CHAPTER 1:
SECRETS OF O.W.C.A.

Welcome to the O.W.C.A. We are the foremost spy agency in the Tri-State Area, dedicated to eradicating (or at least slowing down) the evildoers among us. This chapter will tell you everything you need to know about working with us to fight evil. We *hate* evil.

WHO WE ARE

Major Monogram:

This is Major Francis Monogram. (Yes, his first name is Francis.) He's a bigwig at the agency. He is the immediate supervisor of Agent P, a.k.a. Perry the Platypus. He gives Agent P his assignments each day . . . most of which involve finding out what Dr. Heinz Doofenshmirtz is up to and putting a stop to it.

Three things you should know about Major Monogram:

1) He once dreamed of being an acrobat. Okay, he *still* dreams about it.

2) He's married. Sorry, ladies.

3) His moustache and single eyebrow are completely interchangeable.

WHO WE ARE

Agent P:

He's a semiaquatic, egg-laying mammal of action. What more do you need to know? Well, here are a few "secret" facts about Perry the Platypus, alias Agent P!

1) He is O.W.C.A.'s top agent . . . and, for some reason, is assigned to its least credible threat. (What sense does that make?)

2) His secret identity is the pet platypus of Danville residents Phineas Flynn and Ferb Fletcher. We could go into further detail about his "pet mode," but to be honest, he doesn't do much.

3) He enjoys horseback riding, good books, and long walks on the beach. Perry is also an excellent pachisi player.

** As the top agent for O.W.C.A., Perry's experiences in the field provided much of the material for this book.

WHO ARE *WE*?

Other Key Agents

Although Agent P is the most celebrated, O.W.C.A. would be nothing without its arsenal of animal agents. Here are just a few:

Pinky the Chihuahua:

The nemesis of Professor Poofenplotz, Pinky hides his identity as the jittery pet of Phineas and Ferb's friend Isabella Garcia-Shapiro. His style is shaky at best.

Peter the Panda:

A part-time nemesis of Dr. Doofenshmirtz who resides in Seattle, Peter is cool, cunning, and curiously cuddly.

Terry the Turtle:

Terry the Turtle can appear aloof at first, but once you get to know him, he'll come out of his shell.

Agent G:

Major Monogram once sent Perry the Platypus on a wild goose chase . . . and he found Agent G. He's truly a *fowl* agent.

Agent C:

The only agent who is talented AND tasty over rice.

Agent E:

A high-flier at the agency, he is extremely sensitive. (Don't mention that he's bald.)

WHO ARE *YOU*?

Now that you know all about us, let's find out about you!
We need to know a little something about the people who
want to fight evil. I mean, after all, what if YOU'RE evil?
We can't very well teach you how to fight evil then, can
we? You'd just be fighting yourself.

Your Name: _____ Max _____

Your Age: _____ 9 _____

Are You Evil? (Circle One)   Yes (No) (If "No," then proceed)

Years of School: _____ 5 _____

Years of Spy Training: ___ O _____

The First Time You Encountered Evil (excluding younger
brothers or sisters): ___ Older brother _____

_____

The Most Evil Person in the Movies?: __ an ork __

The Most Evil Person in Books?: ___ Geg _____

Your Hero (Who Fights Evil): __ Percy Jackson Legolas __

Why I Want to Fight Evil (in 29 words or less)(okay, 30 words):

_____

_____

_____

_____

Draw Yourself as an Agent

What would you look like as an official agent of O.W.C.A.?
Fierce and furious? Cool and classy? Eager and egg-laying?
Draw a picture of yourself in the middle of a top secret mission,
kicking some evil butt. And don't forget the fedora!

O.W.C.A.

AGENCY LINGO

Every profession develops its own way of speaking with special words, abbreviations, and catch phrases that mean something to them, but not to the outside world. Nowhere is this more true than in the spy world. What follows are key terms used by O.W.C.A. that every agent needs to know. Study carefully—you will be quizzed later!

AGENCY – Another word for O.W.C.A. Not to be confused with "Agent *C*"—the chicken.

FRIENEMESIS – An adversary with whom you are on friendly terms. (This is the best way to describe Dr. Doofenshmirtz's and Agent P's relationship.)

CODE BLUE – This indicates a serious situation. Not as serious as code red, but *much* more serious than code vermillion.

TUBE JAM – A traffic pileup in the secret agents' pneumatic tube transportation system.

F. A. T. – Fedora Accessible Tools (e.g., "Grab your F. A. T. and let's go!") In this case, Agent P is using a hot dog as his secret weapon!

PRONTO – This means that Major Monogram wants his lunch order right away.

SECRET SPY PAPERWORK

Being a secret agent is not all travel, adventure, and glamour. (If you want that, be a postal worker.)

There is also paperwork. Every agent must fill out a very important form after each mission. But here at O.W.C.A., we try to keep it simple so we can get our agents away from their desks and back on the streets ASAP.

Name: *(Check one)*

Agent _A _B _C _D _E _F _G _H _I _J _K _L ✓M _N
_O _P _Q _R _S _T _U _V _W _X _Y _Z

Today's mission was: *(Check one)* ✓ a success ✓ a failure
✓ it's complicated

I began work today by taking: *(Circle one)* A) a hidden tube
B) a bus   C) a jolly trolly ride . . . **to my lair. I received my
assignment from** A) Major Monogram   B) Admiral Acronym
C) a sickly squirrel . . . **and quickly left to stop my nemesis.**

I burst into the A) secret hideout   B) recreational vehicle   C) gym
locker . . . **of my nemesis and took him by surprise. He managed
to trap me in** A) an ingenious trap   B) an overturned popcorn
bucket   C) a long, awkward conversation about his private life

When he revealed his A) ingenious   B) confusing   C) redecorating
. . . **scheme, I broke free of the trap and** A) defeated my nemesis
B) destroyed his -inator   C) yelled "I'm goin' to Disneyland!"

A) Sincerely,
B) I'm outta here,

Agent M,

(Your Signature Here)

KNOW YOUR LICENSES

Everyone has heard of a "License to Kill," but we don't assign those at O.W.C.A. (Too messy!) However, there ARE many other kinds of licenses you may apply for as an agent.

• **License to Bill** – After a particularly destructive fight with your nemesis, you have the right to bill him for the damages. He'll hate that.

• **License to Quill** – Although most O.W.C.A. forms must be typed or submitted electronically, this allows you to fill them out with an eighteenth century writing quill. (Why you would want to do this is another question entirely.)

• **License to Fish** – This does NOT apply to Agent F, the flounder. If you catch him, please throw him back.

• **License to Floss** – Essential to good hygiene; too many agents overlook this license.

• **License to Blow Up Dangerous -inators** – If you don't have this license, you can always disassemble the -inator piece by piece, but honestly, who has the time for that?

• **License to Grill** – Important if you want a successful summer barbecue. Caution: Before you grill anything, make sure they aren't a fellow agent. We all remember what happened to Agent T last Thanksgiving.

ALL ABOUT . . . "THE ACADEMY"

- Its location is unknown. Its rituals are shrouded in mystery. Its cafeteria food is inedible.

- No one talks about it, but if they do, they do so in hushed whispers.

- It is where every young pup, kitten, and chick learns if it has what it takes to be an agent.

IT IS . . . THE ACADEMY.

MY MEMORIES OF THE ACADEMY

Name: ▓▓▓▓▓

Date: ▓▓▓▓▓▓▓

Locale: ▓▓▓▓▓▓

My first day at ▓▓▓▓▓▓▓ was one etched into my mind forever. Our primary duty was standing at attention while ▓▓▓▓▓▓▓ yelled at us. No matter what he said to us, there were only three acceptable responses:

"Yes, Major."

"No, Major."

"May I get you another cappuccino, Major?"

Any infraction was punished with mandatory ▓▓▓▓▓▓▓ push-ups. We did push-ups in the sun, push-ups in the rain, and we even did push-ups in the snow. And that was just the first day.

When we finally stopped to eat, we were each given one ounce of water, one grain of rice, and, for some reason, all the refried yams we could eat.

At the end of the day, I collapsed into my bunk, exhausted, but secure in the knowledge that in another 729 days I would be a ▓▓▓▓▓▓▓ secret agent.

CLASSES AT . . . "THE ACADEMY"

Education is key at The Academy, second only to pointless discipline, mindless routine, and the destruction of any personal identity. Here is a sample of classes offered each semester.

DEFUSING DEADLY DEVICES

Prerequisite: Ten fingers.

THE ABC'S OF SECRET AGENTING

Action, Brawling, and, strangely enough . . . Calligraphy.

CERAMICS: THE BEAUTY OF BLOBS

Yes, we offer electives. But only one.

RESISTING INTERROGATION

It's much easier if you're an animal that doesn't speak.

ADVANCED CAMOUFLAGE

If we spot you in class, you've already failed.

(MORE) ABOUT . . . "THE ACADEMY"

Life Lessons

Very few agents graduate from the program. You fail instantly if you lose the microfilm, chase your own tail, or bite one of your classmates. But everyone comes out with a sense of empowerment, a host of embarrassing stories, and lifelong lessons . . . lessons like these.

"My most valuable lesson?
Before firing your grappling
hook, make sure it is facing
AWAY from you."
- Agent P

"I learned that a good teacher is
worth more than gold . . . but
Corporal Conundrum can be very
confusing."
- Agent D

"I remember the lesson `Never
trust a spy.' Including me.
So don't believe a word I
just said."
- Agent C

And EVERYONE remembers The Academy motto:
FIGHT LONG. FIGHT STRONG. FIGHT EVIL!

21

MAJOR MONOGRAM'S CORNER: A VIEW FROM THE TOP

I am Major Monogram, the highest-ranking member of the O.W.C.A. Some might call me the *major* major. I oversee all of the really, really important things, the top vital big stuff that goes on here.

Not to diminish the work that Agent P does, but if I wasn't there to send him on his mission, nothing would get done. I mean, *someone* has to tell him, "Dr. Doofenshmirtz is up to something. Put a stop to it." Who's going to do that? Carl? I don't think so!

I'm also responsible for the wallpaper chosen and linens used at O.W.C.A. headquarters. I've gone for a muted palette that I find calming.

CARL'S CORNER: A VIEW FROM THE BOTTOM

Top Ten Tips from the Common Man

1) Be nice to people on the way up because you'll meet them again on the way back down. (I don't know this from personal experience, as I haven't actually moved up yet, but it sounds good.)

2) Paperwork will wait. Major Monogram won't. (Especially for Chinese food!)

3) A penny saved is a penny earned. That's the only penny I've earned so far.

4) When you work with animals, your most important tool is a lint brush.

5) When Major Monogram sunbathes on the O.W.C.A. roof, make sure he uses SPF 75 or he ends up looking like Agent L, the lobster.

6) If you bring gum, you'd better have enough for everyone.

7) Major Monogram likes his coffee with six sugars. Not five. Not seven. *Six.*

8) In the file cabinet, "Agent C" comes after "Agency."

9) Do unto others or you'll get in a lot of trouble!

10) When in doubt, spit it out.

IF I RAN THE O.W.C.A.

What if you were in charge of the O.W.C.A.? What would you do?

I'd hire more: A) humans B) animals C) vegetables D) minerals

I would give all the agents:

A) coffee breaks B) cool weapons C) a raise D) sombreros

I would assign Agent P to deal with: The Same person as before

As for Peter the Panda, I would:

A) fire him B) fight him C) hug him
D) try to comb him . . . he's a mess

And for times when I need a vacation, I would definitely put
_____Agent P,_____ in charge,
because _____responsible._____.

In the O.W.C.A. cafeteria I would serve:

A) healthy alternatives B) mystery meat C) spy pie
D) no one: I'm the boss, why should I serve anybody?

And finally, the new O.W.C.A. motto would be:
_____Subway eat fresh._____

DRAW YOUR OWN HEADQUARTERS

If you were in charge of the O.W.C.A. headquarters (HQ), what would you want it to look like? A tree house? A carnival? A platypus-shaped firehouse? Draw it here!

AGENCY LINGO QUIZ

Okay, you say you want to fight evil and supposedly you've been reading all of our advice so far, but do you *really* remember what you read? Let's see if you can recall the key O.W.C.A. lingo.

WARNING: It's against O.W.C.A. procedures to look back for the answers!

1) What does F.A.T. stand for?

    A) Foreign Agent Transfer

    B) Fedora Accessible Tools

    C) An agent who has put on some holiday weight

2) If you are on good terms with your adversary, he might be called:

    A) A pleasantagonist

    B) Your frienemesis

    C) Buddy

3) What do the letters "HQ" represent?

A) Hypersonic Quotient

B) Hidden Qualifications

C) Headquarters

4) What is "tube jam"?

A) An improvised song played by agents on the subway

B) The squeezable jelly Carl puts on Major Monogram's sandwiches

C) A pneumatic tube traffic pileup

5) Why did the agent cross the road?

A) To get to the other side

B) Because it was a dangerous code blue situation

C) This is no time for riddles! Get serious!

(Answers on page 142)

As an agent, your every movement is examined and analyzed, your missions reviewed and evaluated. It is essential for each operative to know how to effectively deal with criticism. Here are some helpful tips!

Do listen respectfully.
Do *not* throw your chair at the screen.

Do take notes if the critique is detailed.
Do *not* draw your superior as a goat.

Do make every attempt to learn from your mistakes.
Do *not* quit and go join L.O.V.E.M.U.F.F.I.N. (League of Villainous Evildoers Maniacally United for Frightening Investments in Naughtiness.)

CHAPTER 2:
SECRET AGENT 411

These skilled operatives are the front line in the battle against evildoers. They are the few, the proud, the animals. Welcome to the world of the secret agent!

HOW TO LOOK LIKE AN AGENT

If you are going to represent the O.W.C.A., you need to maintain a certain image. That said, here are tips for the fashion-forward agent on the go.

- Always comb your hair, fur, or feathers, as the case may be.

- Trim nails if you have them. Buff your hooves. Brush your fangs.

- The most important agent accessory is his hat. While creativity is nice, we strongly advocate the traditional fedora.

- We are NOT fans of casual Fridays. Save it for the beach!

HOW *NOT* TO LOOK LIKE AN AGENT: DISGUISES AND CAMOUFLAGE

While it is important to project a professional image when you are TRYING to look like an agent, it can be even more important at times to NOT look like one. When you are going undercover, spying for secret intelligence, or trying to avoid a bill collector, that's when disguises and camouflage are key.

Can you spot the hidden agent?

A simple accessory makes all the difference.

Even the most brilliant nemesis wouldn't suspect that this is a secret agent in disguise!

The old zip-up Ferb Fletcher disguise.

Stay hidden *and* seasonally appropriate!

However, there is such a thing as going *too* far.

AGENT P TRIVIA

How much do you know about O.W.C.A.'s best agent? Take this quiz and test your knowledge!

1) What was the original name of Perry the Platypus?

A) P to the P B) P Squared C) Bartholomew D) Stinky Jim

2) How many times has Agent P defeated Dr. Doofenshmirtz?

A) 50 B) 100 C) Over 150 D) 8,736,543

3) Who else has Agent P defeated besides Dr. Doofenshmirtz?

A) Dr. Diminutive B) The Regurgitator
C) Dennis the Rogue Rabbit Agent D) All of the above

4) Agent P from the 2nd Dimension was turned into:

A) A platysaurus B) A platyborg C) A platypult
D) A sandwich

5) Dr. Doofenshmirtz made duplicates of Perry the Platypus and one survived. What was its name?

A) Crab Cake Joe B) Jerry C) Francisco de Palma
D) Mary the Platypus

BONUS QUESTION

If you were driving Agent P 478 miles from another city to his lair at 63 miles per hour for the first 35 minutes, and at 86 miles per hour for the rest of the trip, not including a very necessary rest stop, what color were the driver's eyes?

(Answers on page 142)

EVEN AGENTS GET SICK

It's regrettable, but it happens. Agents get sick. More often than not they catch something from an unsanitary nemesis.

When an agent is home sick with a cold or flu, it's up to backup agents to fill in. (Think substitute teachers with lethal ninja skills.) Several have stepped in to fight Dr. Doofenshmirtz when Agent P was unavailable.

Agent S
Slow but crafty, this snail agent is small, powerful, and makes excellent escargot.

Agent R
Bulky, cumbersome, and heavy, Agent R is a real heavyweight as an opponent.

A Random Platypus

Although not *technically* an agent, this escaped zoo animal managed to defeat Dr. Doofenshmirtz in record time.

Planty the Potted Plant

Despite not being an animal, or even a thinking creature, this plant stopped Dr. Doofenshmirtz anyway and was awarded honorary agent status.

Every agent needs a code name, a name that they use in the field. Each organization determines these undercover monikers in their own way. For example, the British branch assigns numbers like Agent Double 00. The animal branch of O.W.C.A. assigns letters like Agent P and Agent D. For human agents, it's a little more complicated.

First, write down the name of your first pet:

Moofis
.

Now, write down the name of the first street you lived on:

Allen
.

Put the two words together and that's your secret agent code name!

Moofi Allen
.

Are you Pinky Ventura?
Nimbus El Centro? Goldie
Champs-Élysées? Or even
Mr.Fluffypants Broadway?
Whatever your name, no
one will ever suspect
that it's you.

AGENT P'S TO DO LIST

Ripped directly from the notebook of O.W.C.A.'s number-one agent, this "To Do" list from Agent P should give you a perfect look into the typical day of a secret agent.

1) Get up.

2) Floss.

3) Go to the lair (in a unique way if possible).

4) Get assignment.

5) Stop nemesis.

6) Destroy -inator.

7) Pick up dry cleaning.

8) Make platypus noise when host family says, "Oh, there you are, Perry!"

SECRET AGENT HEALTH

Fighting evil requires fast reflexes and strong bones, so eating right is essential. This is one of Major Monogram's favorite recipes.

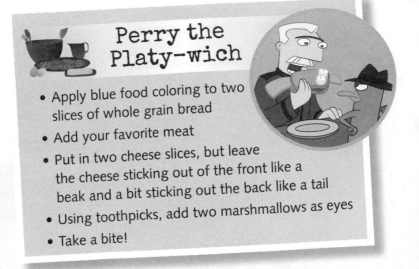

Perry the Platy-wich

- Apply blue food coloring to two slices of whole grain bread
- Add your favorite meat
- Put in two cheese slices, but leave the cheese sticking out of the front like a beak and a bit sticking out the back like a tail
- Using toothpicks, add two marshmallows as eyes
- Take a bite!

Or, if your adversary is coming over, try serving up one of these:

Nemesis Knuckle Sandwich

- Take one nemesis
- Add some punch
- Keep on low heat until nemesis rises
- Whip into frenzy
- Beat until soft
- Break into bite-size chunks and serve

SECRET AGENT EXERCISE

Secret agents also need exercise to stay in top physical condition. Did you know that fighting enemies can burn 500 calories an hour? Here's the skinny:

Exercise	Calories burned
Putting on a fedora	5
Sliding into your lair	10
Hitting a nemesis	10
Hitting a nemesis twice	20
Busting out of a trap	20
Breaking through a wall	25
Platy-push-ups	30
Platy-pull-ups	30
Marmoset-ups	35
Jumping jack-rabbits	40
Yak yoga	50
Cheesy 1980's exercise video	150

HOW TO WORK WITH ANOTHER SECRET AGENT

There are times where agents must team up to thwart a particularly evil character (like a reality TV star!). So, you'll need to know the rules for working with a partner.

1) Never share fedoras. It's just not sanitary.

2) Never fall for the same person (or animal) that your partner likes. Very messy.

3) When you're about to go into battle with your partner, never say "I'm too old for this" or "I'm one week from retirement." You're just asking for trouble.

It's also important to remember the differences between working solo and working with a partner:

	Solo	Partnered
During a stakeout	Play solitaire while you wait.	Play rock, paper, scissors while you wait.
Chasing a villain	Take the fastest vehicle possible.	Take the car pool lane. Ride sharing helps us all.
Ordering take-out	Get a small pizza.	Split a large and save, save, save!

IMAGINE YOURSELF AS THE PERFECT AGENT

As you strive to become the best secret agent you can, it can help to visualize yourself the way you want to be. Picture yourself with the best skills and traits of all your favorite operatives.

1) If you could have any platypus ability, which would you want?

A) The ability to lay eggs

B) A venomous spur

C) Waterproof fur

D) Semiaquaticness

2) Which Perry ability would you prefer?

A) Platyjitsu

B) Guitar playing

C) DJing

D) The ability to blend in with teal wallpaper

3) Which Perry device would you want in your arsenal?

A) A spinning fedora saw

B) An auto-scan replicator

C) A paraglider

D) An automatic toenail clipper

4) What skill from another agent would you choose?

A) Peter the Panda's stealth

B) Pinky the Chihuahua's good looks

C) Agent E's wings

D) Agent G's height

5) If you could have a power that NO agent has, which would you want?

A) Invisibility

B) Super strength

C) Fingers that shoot bananas

D) The ability to talk

YOUR THEME SONG

Every agent needs a theme song. It makes your nemesis nervous and it gives you something to hum while you're fighting. Write your own agent theme song below.

Start simple. First, write new lyrics to a tune you already know. Here's an example:

> *I'm a semi-bionic, ball-playing kid who's relaxin'.*
> *A redheaded agent who never fails to be brave.*
> *I wear a coat of camouflage,*
> *With a lair in Mom's garage,*
> *And the villains are doomed whenever I'm on my way!*
> *I'm Jerry. Jerry the eight-year-old!*

Now you try it. First, think of a song you know well:

_____

Now change the lyrics so they are all about you:

_____

_____

_____

_____

Try to have the same number of syllables in each line as the original song. Here's one about a new agent to another tune.

> *I'm an agent, it's true.*
> *All my training is through.*
> *But my mouse head's so little . . .*
> *My fedora's askew.*

Pick another song, maybe a different style altogether:

_____

Now change the lyrics so they are about you on a dangerous spy mission:_____

_____

_____

_____

_____

Here's another tip: Sometimes it helps to think of the rhyme and work backward. Otherwise you'll find yourself stuck trying to rhyme something with *platypus* or *Doofenshmirtz.* Good luck with that!_____

_____

_____

Now for your own official secret agent theme song. What's your favorite song?_____

Now write new lyrics to that song about your secret agent abilities:_____

_____

_____

_____

_____

AGENT AUDITIONS

At an agency as accomplished as O.W.C.A., we get a lot of young recruits who want to be secret agents. But are they ready? You be the judge. (Circle one answer.)

1) Agent material?

Yes   No

2) Ready to fight evil?

Yes   No

3) Good enough for O.W.C.A.?
Yes   No

4) Prepared to be a spy?
Yes   No

5) Qualified to kick butt?
Yes   No

6) Old enough to have a nemesis?
Yes   No

(Answers on page 142)

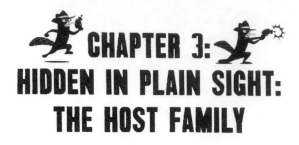

CHAPTER 3:
HIDDEN IN PLAIN SIGHT:
THE HOST FAMILY

Every O.W.C.A. agent is given a secret identity, posing as the common, everyday pet of a host family. But the host family can never know that their dog or cat or naked mole rat is actually a secret agent.

An agent spends a great deal of time with his or her family and it's important to learn as much about them, and how to deal with them, as possible. Are they social butterflies or disgruntled loners? Friendly animal lovers or selfish caretakers? You need to know.

In the case of Perry the Platypus, his host family is the Flynn-Fletcher family. They are the nicest family in Danville!

PHINEAS FLYNN

Inventive, creative, and several other words ending in "ive"

Can recognize Perry out of dozens of other platypuses

Often says "Where's Perry?" and "Oh, there you are, Perry."

Loving caretaker of his pet

Helped Perry to become a spokesmodel (not sure what this has to do with his knee)

FERB FLETCHER

Can smell when Perry needs a bath from fifty paces (peeyew!)

Thinks Perry doesn't do much. Which is okay, because Ferb doesn't say much.

Would build Perry a bed or house or intergalactic hovercraft out of cheese . . . *if* he needed it.

Once walked for miles to find his missing pet.

LAWRENCE FLETCHER

- Phineas and Ferb's dad
- Antiquer and shop owner
- Married a former pop star
- Big fan of Pinhead Pierre

LINDA FLYNN-FLETCHER

- Phineas and Ferb's mom
- Homemaker, but oddly enough, rarely home
- Involved in seventy-eight different clubs, classes, and projects
- Buys all the groceries, including pet food for Perry!

CANDACE FLYNN

- Phineas and Ferb's older sister
- WARNING: May try to bathe pet to impress a boy
- WARNING: May trip over pet at night
- WARNING: May run, yell, or scream with no warning

HOW TO GET ADOPTED BY A GOOD FAMILY

As an agent, the family you are placed with will determine where you live, what you eat, and whether you have to wear tutus and tiaras, so it is preferable to get adopted by a good family. Here are some rules to help make that a reality.

DO make eye contact with prospective families.

DON'T make physical contact with your fists.

DO try to look adorable.

DON'T break out of your cage and blow up their -inators.

DO show off by making a cute sound or wiggling your ears.

DON'T show off by karate chopping someone and saving the world.

Remember: You could end up with a family like this! ➡️

52

HOW TO HIDE YOUR SECRET IDENTITY

As mentioned earlier, your host family can never find out that you are actually a secret agent. If they do find out (even after we just told you that they can never find out), well, then, their minds will be erased or you will be shipped away, never to see them again. To keep that from happening, here are:

Five Tips for Appearing to Be a Mindless Pet

1) Don't do much.

2) Stay on all fours.

3) If possible, drool.

4) Try to look in two directions at the same time.

5) Drool some more.

IF YOUR IDENTITY IS ENDANGERED

Even the most diligent agent can have close calls, and sometimes you'll come dangerously close to revealing your secret identity to your host family. In drastic cases, you may have to resort to one of these last-ditch tactics:

Destroy all evidence, adopt a disguise, and hop the first flight to Siberia.

Set off a local volcano and hope everyone forgets about you.

Give them an informative pamphlet. It's helpful!

HOW TO SNEAK AWAY SUCCESSFULLY

It's a fact of life: you can't fight evil if you're stuck at home with your host family. So you need to know how to slip away at a moment's notice.

HIDE

- Behind a tree.
- In the chimney.
- Against a teal painting.

USE A DISTRACTION

- Wait for a passing parade, traveling circus, or fireworks display.
- Call for a pizza. When the delivery guy rings the doorbell and everyone is distracted, run.
- Throw a rock.

USE A DECOY

- A log under the arm will pacify a sleeping child.
- A teal loaf of bread will fool the average housewife.

- A Perry the Platypus inaction figure looks good at a distance of fifty feet or more!

Let's get your creative juices flowing with something we at the agency like to call "Tell Your Own Story." (Which should have been clear from the heading at the top of the page.) Examine these pictures from one of Agent P's missions and write your own descriptions under each picture to tell a whole new story about what you think is going on.

....

....

....

....

....

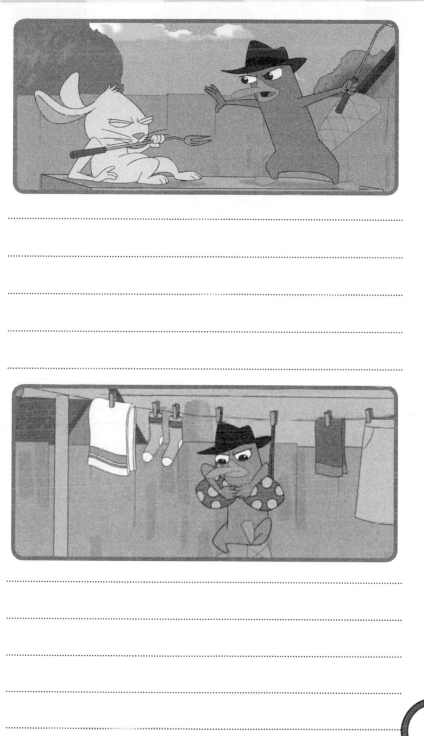

....

....

....

....

....

....

....

....

HOW TO PROTECT YOUR FAMILY

It's sad, but true. Sometimes your high-stakes, death-defying, action-filled, super-spy life may put your host family in danger . . . and it's up to you to protect them! Here's how.

Take the Fight to the Nemesis
Don't fight where you live. Fight at the lair of your nemesis. That way, no matter who gets hurt or what gets broken, it will be his.

Dome It
Put a clear Plexiglas dome over your entire house for protection. This is highly effective, but not always practical if your host family likes to, you know, leave the house occasionally.

Buckle Up
Get your host family to fasten their seat belts. Okay, it doesn't have anything to do with evil, but come on. It's just common sense.

Move It
If your nemesis keeps accidentally hitting your host family with his -inator blasts, day after day after day, why don't you turn the -inators in another direction? ANY other direction!

Smoke Detectors

Come on. It costs what, twenty bucks? You can buy this book, but you can't blow twenty on a smoke detector?

Avoid Incredibly Dangerous Situations

If you know downtown Danville will be covered in evil gelatin or carnivorous potatoes that afternoon, subtly influence your family to go elsewhere for the day.

PERRY TO THE RESCUE!

A FILL-IN-THE-BLANK ADVENTURE

Part of being a secret agent is dealing with incomplete information. You may know part of someone's evil plan, but you'll have to make educated guesses to fill in the blanks. Fill in the blanks below with crazy words to complete this high-stakes mission.

Agent P crashed through the roof of _The "Mall_
PLACE

where the _____ Dr. Doofenshmirtz had been
ADJECTIVE

working on a _____-inator.
ADJECTIVE

"Ah, Perry the Platypus!" Dr. Doofenshmirtz said

_____. "What a _____ surprise. And by
ADVERB   ADJECTIVE

that, I mean a surprise for YOU!" The evil doctor trapped

Perry in a _____ and tried to _____ on his skiff
NOUN   VERB

and fly away with his -inator. But Perry broke out and grabbed

the skiff's _____ and held on tight. Flying high over
NOUN

the _____, Agent P pulled himself aboard and
NOUN

_____ attacked Dr. Doofenshmirtz. Perry kicked the
ADVERB

_____ doctor into the -inator and it fired, making
ADJECTIVE

a _____ huge _____! The -inator blast
ADJECTIVE   SOUND EFFECT

shot down into the backyard of Phineas and _____,
                                            NAME OF A PERSON

hitting Ferb. Suddenly, Ferb turned into a _____! A
                                           ANIMAL

second _____ blast began to _____ Phineas
       ADJECTIVE   VERB

into a half- _____ half- _____!
             ANIMAL   NOUN

Perry knew he had to help them . . . and _____!
                                         ADVERB

Quickly pulling a _____ from his fedora, Perry used
                  NOUN

it to _____ Doofenshmirtz.
      VERB

" _____!" Dr. Doofenshmirtz cried as he fell off
  EXCLAMATION

the skiff and into a pile of _____. Perry hit the reverse
                             PLURAL NOUN

switch on the evil doctor's _____ -inator
                            ADJECTIVE

and _____ changed the boys back to normal. And
    ADVERB

by normal, we mean _____.
                   ADJECTIVE

THE END.

SECRET AGENT: MIA

Sometimes an agent goes missing in action. To their host family, that means a lost pet. If you are that lost pet, here's what to do.

1) Don't panic! Use the GPS (Global Positioning System) device in your fedora to find your location. (Although, if you still had that, I guess you wouldn't be lost. Never mind.)

2) If you see a "Missing Pet" poster with a picture of your face, do NOT call the phone number on it. Yes, you want to be found, but not at the expense of your secret identity, and as soon as they hear you on the phone, they'll know something is up. I mean, for one, how did a pet dial their number?!?

3) Listen carefully. Often times, the youngest members of the host family will compose a song, set up a sound system, and then sing across the whole city to find you. If they do, just waddle on up. Problem solved!

REST AND RELAXATION ZONE

Even Agent P needs some well-deserved rest and relaxation to unwind from the high-stress lifestyle of a secret agent, so we hereby order you to rest and relax with the following jokes.

What does Dr. Doofenshmirtz wear under his jackets?

Doofen-*shirts*

Which agent has the most experience battling pirates?

Agent Rrrrrrr

What is a secret agent's favorite bug?

A *spy*-der

CHAPTER 4:
EVIL PERSONIFIED: YOUR NEMESIS

A hero is defined by his nemesis. If there were no evil to fight, then a hero would have nothing to do and would end up sitting around all day, watching TV, eating junk food, and making prank phone calls. And what kind of hero is that? So this chapter is devoted to the bane of your existence: your nemesis!

Do You Know Your Nemesis?

Perry's nemesis is the not-quite-infamous Dr. Heinz Doofenshmirtz. How much do you know about Danville's least-successful evil scientist?

- Dr. Heinz Doofenshmirtz was born in the city of Gimmelshtoomp in the Eastern European country of Druselstein. His parents did not attend his birth.

- Dr. Doofenshmirtz is famous for inventing -inators, but he's also made a *not*-inator, a robot named Norm, a Bo-at, Eulg, Doofania, and a Shinkspheria. He also makes a mean three-bean casserole.

DOOF LOVES:

- Almond brittle
- Limburger cheese
- Vanessa (Vanessa is his daughter. He really loves her, although he wishes she would enjoy being evil.)

DOOF HATES:

Barking dogs

Bellhops

Bird songs

Birthdays

Blinking traffic arrows

Ear hair (Understandable)

Golf

Hot dog vendors

Kittens (Wha?!?)

Lawn gnomes

Meter maids

Mimes (Who doesn't?)

Musical instruments that start with "B"

Pelicans

Public pools

Rice pudding

Sandwich-board guys

Sports fans

Taxi drivers

Tony's Deli

Underwater welders

Yoga teachers

FROM THE NEMESIS: A REBUTTAL

OKAY, WAIT WAIT WAIT WAIT
WAIT WAIT! WAIT. WAIT.

THERE HAS BEEN A WHOLE LOT SAID IN THIS BOOK
ABOUT EVIL, BUT WHO'S SAYING IT? A BUNCH OF
GOOD GUYS WHO HAVE NEVER BEEN EVIL! IT'S RIDICULOUS!

THE ENTIRE PREMISE OF THIS BOOK IS THAT YOU CAN FIGHT AND
SOMEHOW DEFEAT EVIL?!?? BUT EVIL CAN'T BE DEFEATED! I MEAN,
YES, TECHNICALLY, PERRY THE PLATYPUS DEFEATS EVIL EVERY DAY,
DAY AFTER DAY, 24-7-365 DAYS A YEAR BUT IN THE BROADER SENSE,
IN THE SYMBOLIC SENSE, YOU CAN'T STOP EVIL!

SO I'M GOING TO KEEP ON KEEPIN' ON!

(I'M HEINZ DOOFENSHMIRTZ AND I APPROVE THIS MESSAGE.)

When you look evil in the eyes day after day, sometimes you have to take a step back and laugh at it. Here are Perry's favorite jokes about his evil nemesis.

Where does Heinz keep his chickens?
In a chicken *coop*enshmirtz

Why did Dr. Doofenshmirtz get wet whenever it rained? **He had a hole in the *roof*enshmirtz**

What does the evil doctor eat when he has a cold? **Chicken noodle *soup*enshmirtz**

What did Heinz call his dentist?
Dr. Poole A. *Tooth*enshmirtz

TEN WAYS TO TELL IF YOUR NEIGHBOR IS AN EVIL VILLAIN

1) He just has that evil look. You know the one.

2) He waters his lawn too much.

3) He keeps talking about ruling the Tri-State Area.

4) He doesn't smile enough.

5) He smiles *too* much.

6) He builds strange devices called -inators.

7) He borrows things and forgets to give them back. (My lawn can't mow itself, you know!)

8) He curses animals when they defeat him.

9) He leaves his trash cans on the street for days at a time.

10) His business card has the word "evil" on it.

HOW TO ENDURE LONG, RAMBLING BACKSTORIES

So, your nemesis loves to talk. That's just a fact of life. He'll start out telling you how his mother deprived him of citrus as a youth, and consequently the emotional toll, not to mention the lack of vitamin C, has forced him to steal lemons thirty years later. He'll moan about how *this person* wronged him and *that person* ignored him until finally he's just rambling about how cassette mix tapes "totally ruled."

So when your nemesis inevitably launches into a long, rambling backstory, you can either let it drive you nuts or you can put that time to good use.

1) File your nails. (If you have nails.)

2) Compose a grocery list in your head. (Don't forget milk.)

3) Look for subtle clues in the backstory that reveal your enemy's debilitating weakness.

4) Sing songs to yourself. Your favorite *Phineas and Ferb* song would be a good choice!

5) Plot your escape. Go ahead. He's not paying attention.

6) See how many words you can make out of the letters in the phrase "Doof is a doofus."

7) Imagine your nemesis wearing an old-timey bathing suit.

8) Keep a crossword puzzle in your fedora to help pass the time.

9) Practice your spitting. (Distance and accuracy!)

10) Count how many unusual sounds you can make with your body parts.

FRIENEMESIS: NAVIGATING THE FRIEND / ENEMY DIVIDE

When you work with someone for a long time you have a tendency to become friends . . . even if that person is your enemy. Befriending your nemesis is a slippery slope and caring too much can be your downfall. But with a few helpful tips, you can navigate the frienemesis waters with confidence.

ALWAYS – Be courteous and polite.

SOMETIMES – Assist with small tasks.

NEVER – Agree to help him move to a new place. C'mon. Hire a moving company, ya cheapskate!

ALWAYS – Acknowledge birthdays and holidays.

SOMETIMES – Send a card.

NEVER – Send holiday cards together with pictures of the two of you in matching sweaters. Yuck!

ALWAYS – Offer to pay for your half of a meal.

SOMETIMES – Offer to treat.

NEVER – Pay his rent. Just say no.

WHAT TO DO WHEN YOUR NEMESIS IS DOWNGRADED

It can happen to the best of us . . . but more often to the worst of us. Being downgraded is part of life, especially if you are a lame evil scientist. It happened to Dr. Doofenshmirtz once, and so Perry was reassigned to a more dangerous nemesis. Here's how to cope if it happens to *your* lame evil scientist.

DON'T TAKE IT PERSONALLY

It's not about you, it's about your foe. In fact, it may be BECAUSE you are so successful in defeating him time and time again that he is considered so horribly lame.

BE SUPPORTIVE OF YOUR NEMESIS

He's got to be feeling bad about this setback. Don't remind him of how unsuccessful he is and try to avoid phrases like "complete disappointment" and "total failure." Send him a gift instead!

BE PREPARED FOR CHANGE

You may be transferred to a more formidable foe, so be ready. I mean, seriously, anybody would be more formidable than the one you've been battling.

HOW TO ESCAPE FROM TRAPS

Villains like using traps. That's a given. So if you're going to fight evil, you're going to spend time in your fair share of traps and will need to know the best way out.

Chinese Platypus Trap:
Make friends with someone who has a pair of scissors.

Bubble of Pure Evil:
Befriend a beaver with a toothpick. (Not as simple.)

Egg Trap:
Use your beak to peck your way to freedom. You *do* have a beak, don't you?

Tied to a Birthday Firecracker:

Use your watch laser to burn through your bonds just before they sing "Happy Birthday" and light those candles.

Biodegradable Box:

Leap in front of the beam of a Rotten-inator, then dramatically break through the rotting container. (It's the "dramatically" part that's key!)

The Indoors-inator-Trap:

Use your tail to knock on the door and wait for your easily fooled nemesis to open it. Surprise!

Straitjacket:

Sometimes the most obvious answers are the right ones. Use your grappling hook to shoot a vengeful robot as it races by and then pull yourself loose. See? Obvious!

CAN YOU IDENTIFY THESE -INATORS?

The -inator! The most diabolical of all evil devices. They come in all shapes, sizes, and flavors, and it is up to you to be able to identify them at a moment's notice. Can you match the -inator names below to the corresponding picture?

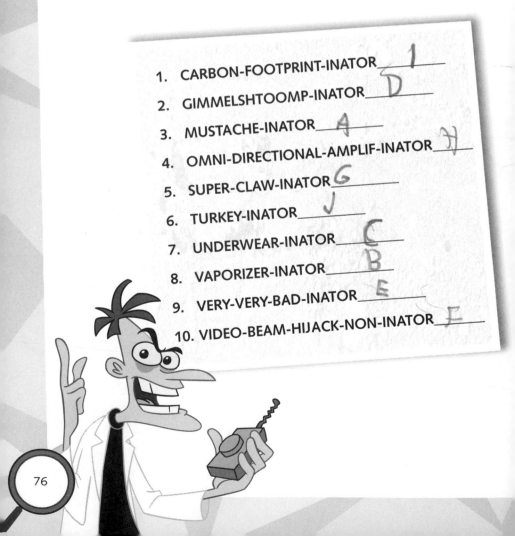

1. CARBON-FOOTPRINT-INATOR __I__
2. GIMMELSHTOOMP-INATOR __D__
3. MUSTACHE-INATOR __A__
4. OMNI-DIRECTIONAL-AMPLIF-INATOR __H__
5. SUPER-CLAW-INATOR __G__
6. TURKEY-INATOR __J__
7. UNDERWEAR-INATOR __C__
8. VAPORIZER-INATOR __B__
9. VERY-VERY-BAD-INATOR __E__
10. VIDEO-BEAM-HIJACK-NON-INATOR __F__

(Answers on page 142)

WHAT TO DO IF YOU ARE -INATORED!

Sometimes it happens. You are hit by an -inator beam. But if you don't panic and remember this training, you just may be okay.

If your nemesis uses an **AGE-ACCELERATOR-INATOR** to turn you into an octogenarian, there is an easy remedy. Simply put on an Age-Accelerator-inator-proof suit BEFORE you get hit with the -inator.

When you are hit by a **DANCE-INATOR**, you have no choice but to dance. You can, however, choose WHAT dance you do. Start a conga line and lead that -inator right off the edge of the building. Kaboom!

The only way to escape the static cling of the **STATIC-ELECTRIC-AMPLIF-INATOR** is to wait for several hundred balloons to pull you from the wall. Don't worry, it'll happen.

If you're the victim of the **PLATY-PROLIFERATOR-INATOR**, your only hope is to fight off the endless platoons of robotic platypi one by one until you can suck them back into the -inator like evil dust motes into an evil vacuum.

So you've been hit by a **DE-EVOLUTION-INATOR!** Now what? Well, try to reduce your nemesis to a single-celled organism, and you'll soon find you have the upper hand. Actually, you'll have the *only* hands.

When your nemesis controls you with a **DE-EVOLITION-INATOR** (not to be confused with the de-evolution-inator), struggle to resist until your host family takes control of you with a video-game controller and orders you to knock your nemesis into next Sunday.

**When in doubt, look on the -inator for a self-destruct button. It may seem obvious, but you'd be surprised how many times supposed evil "geniuses" install these on everything they build.

-INATOR BUILDING 101

You may know how to destroy an -inator, but do you know how to BUILD one? On more than one occasion, Perry the Platypus has had to reconstruct a broken -inator to right a wrong. Here's a step-by-step guide to lead you through it.

1. Cover your area with a drop cloth.

2. Lay out the parts and make sure no pieces are missing.

3. Don safety goggles and ankle pads.

4. Insert Tab A into Slot B.

5. Turn screws counterclockwise to tighten.

6. Ask Mom or Dad to help cut on the dotted line with safety scissors.

7. Press wooden dowels into predrilled holes.

8. Slide the gear shaft into the conducting rod.

9. Rotate the propeller until the rubber band is taut.

10. Stand back and admire your newly completed -inator.

REPURPOSING EVIL

Although Dr. Doofenshmirtz's -inators were all designed for evil, many of them could also be used for good. How would you use these inventions to do something good?

The Combin-inator: Besides peanut butter and chocolate, what would you combine and why?_____ _____ _____

The Mind-Transfer-inator: You could switch the minds of your dentist and the ice cream man . . . then you'd get tutti-frutti at every six-month appointment! Who would you switch minds with and why?_____ _____ _____ _____

The Other-Dimension-inator: Could access to other worlds help mankind? Where would you go and why?_____ _____ _____ _____

The Forgetabout-it-inator:
You might make your parents
forget that bad report card. Is there
anything you'd like to forget? _____

_____

_____

_____

The Least-Likely-inator: It makes people
do the thing they would normally be the
least likely to do . . . like eat lima beans!
Is there anyone who deserves to be
blasted with it? What would they do?

_____

_____

_____

_____

The Go-Away-inator: Not for
use on little brothers and sisters.
What would the world be better
without and why? _____

_____

_____

_____

The Duplic-8-Inator: Is there anything
(like Saturdays!) that we could use eight
times as much of? Write them here!

_____

_____

_____

_____

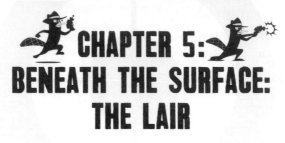

CHAPTER 5:
BENEATH THE SURFACE:
THE LAIR

If you want to be a successful secret agent, you'll need a hidden lair complete with all the tools of the trade.

PERRY'S LAIR DISSECTED

Here is a prime example of a state-of-the-art secret agent lair. Look and learn.

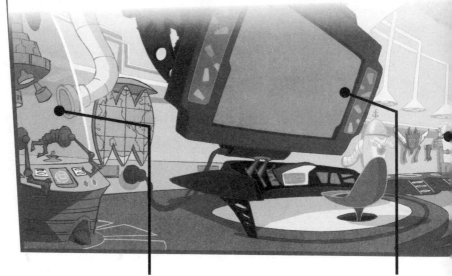

ISOLATION CHAMBER
Using the artificial arms beneath this protective dome, Perry can manipulate and examine any object or element without fear of contamination, radiation, *or* exfoliation.

MAJOR MONOGRAM MONITOR
Also known as the M.M.M., this massive monitor is where Agent P receives his assignments, updates, and sometimes winning lotto numbers.

ALL-TERRAIN BATTLE SUITS

Agent P is prepared for whatever environment he encounters, whether it be the vacuum of space, the intense pressures of the ocean floor, or the peer pressure of a masquerade ball.

HYDRAULIC LIFT

Perry can enter and exit his lair through this high-powered lift that connects to the Flynn-Fletcher chimney. (It's specifically programmed NOT to play elevator music.)

HOVER CAR

Just one of many secret agent vehicles at Agent P's disposal, this car can go from 0 to 60 in 3.2 seconds. (It can also go to the mall in 5.3 seconds, but there's never any parking, so he usually just turns around.)

TRI-TANK AREA

Dr. Doofenshmirtz may occasionally forget that Perry the Platypus is semiaquatic, but Perry's lair is equipped with three tanks for all his water needs: salt, fresh, and carbonated.

DETECTING HIDDEN LAIR ENTRANCES

In an emergency, you may have to find the nearest lair entrance ASAP. Can you find all eight?

(Answers on page 142)

DRAW A COOL LAIR ENTRANCE

Perry has entered his lair through trees, pictures, garden hoses—you name it! What would your ideal lair entrance look like? Draw it below!

THE TROUBLE WITH TUBES

As anyone who follows Agent P's adventures can attest, the O.W.C.A. pneumatic-tube system is not without its problems. Traffic jams. Mistaken detours. Elephants stuck in mouse-sized passages. It's not always easy to get where you're going. Can you find the tube that leads to Perry's lair?

(Answers on page 142)

FINISH THIS MISSION BRIEFING

Major Monogram has important instructions for Agent P, but there is an O.W.C.A. malfunction! Help him finish giving Agent P the important information!

HELLO, AGENT P. SORRY FOR CALLING YOU IN SO EARLY TODAY, BUT IT'S AN EMERGENCY.

ACCORDING TO THIS MESSAGE FROM CARL, DR. DOOFENSHMIRTZ HAS TURNED THE ENTIRE POPULATION OF THE TRI-STATE AREA INTO RATS!

ON HIS BOOKSHELF: REQUIRED READING

Take a look at the bookshelf in Agent P's lair. He has collected all of the essential books that every agent should read. What are some of your favorite books? Write them here.

_____

_____

_____

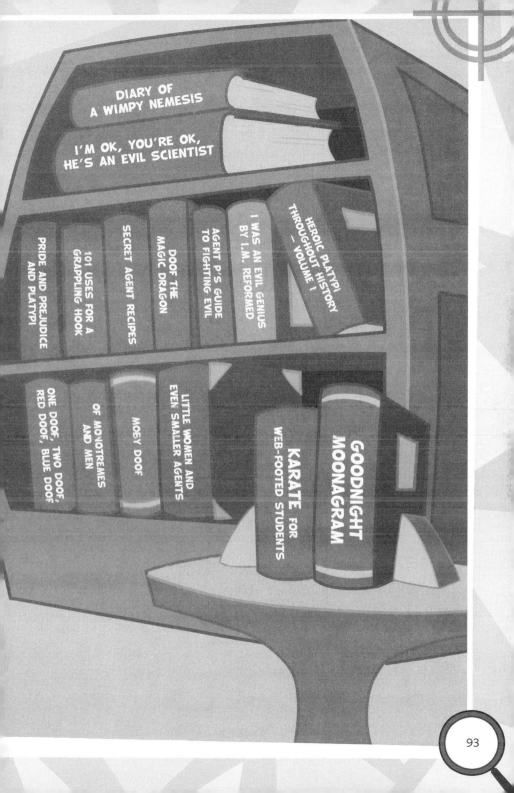

CHAPTER 6: TOOLS OF THE TRADE

A secret agent relies on a razor-sharp mind, finely tuned muscles, and a rigorous training schedule. And when those don't work, he turns to cool gadgets.

KNOW YOUR EQUIPMENT:

The spy watch: This essential communication device allows audio and video contact with O.W.C.A. and other agents, 24-7. (But don't call Major Monogram between 3:30 and 4:00. That's when he showers.)

You know Danville like the back of your hand, but when your assignment takes you to the greater Tri-State Area or beyond, a map and compass will help you stay on course. (If you have a GPS, then just ignore this one.)

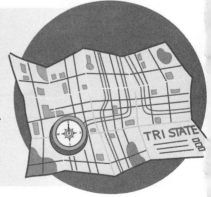

The Piton Gun (or Explosive Bolt Grappling Hook Launch Mechanism) is essential when falling, climbing, swinging, or when you just want to shoot something heavy at Doof's head.

Don't want anyone to know you've been sneaking around? These fake feet make fake footprints to fool your foul foe!

Let's face it, a villain like Dr. Doofenshmirtz isn't very secretive. He'll come right out and tell you his location, his scheme, and the combination to his safe. But traditional spy equipment such as a listening bug or a hidden camera can be very helpful when your nemesis isn't that . . . uh . . . dumb.

THE FEDORA DISSECTED

Agent P's fedora isn't just a stylish hat. It's got many important hidden spy gadgets.

WHISTLES
When your watch-phone isn't an option, call the nearest animal or animal agent with these handy whistles. (Note: *Don't* use the whale whistle unless you want a serious mess.)

A PAD AND PENCIL
These are vital for writing down clues, notes, assignments, and other agents' fast-food orders.

A HOT DOG
This can be used both as an emergency snack *and* as a fencing weapon.

LOCK PICKS

Not every door is as flimsy as Dr. Doofenshmirtz's doors, so if you can't knock it down, a lock pick will get you in quick.

A BAR CODE

When scanned, this hidden magnetic strip allows access to the O.W.C.A. mainframe—and to Major Monogram's private video-game collection!

AN AUTOSCAN REPLICATION DEVICE

This device scans -inators and other inventions so they can be re-created at a later date.

A BUZZ SAW

The fedora contains a motor that, when activated, spins the hat brim like a circular saw. Good for destroying -inators and for trimming hedges.

DESIGN YOUR OWN VEHICLE

Perry travels by jet pack, hover car, moped, helicopter, parachute, and hang glider, but how do YOU roll? Or fly? Or bounce? Create and draw your own unique methods of spy transportation.

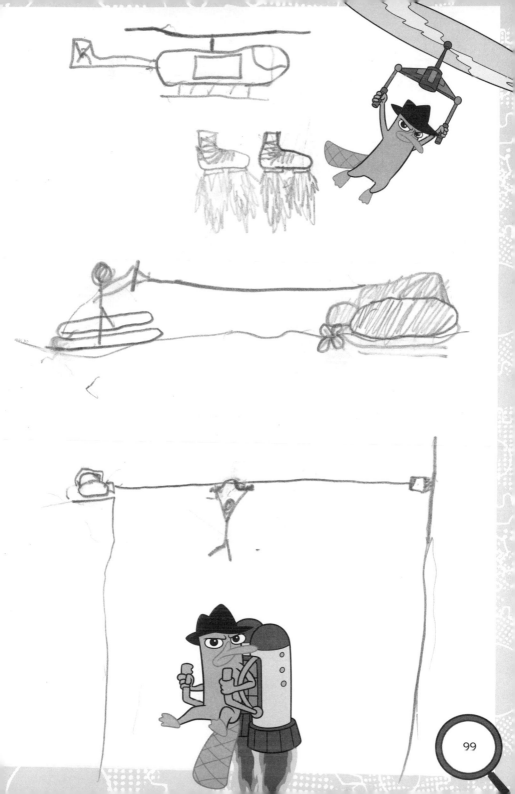

THE RIGHT TOOL FOR THE JOB

Perry has always managed to thwart Dr. Doofenshmirtz and he does it in his own inimitable way. But that doesn't mean it's the *only* way. Take a look at what Perry used in each situation and then draw the secret agent equipment you would use and how you'd use it to save the day!

Perry once used a blender to chop up an -inator.

What device would you use to destroy Dr. Doofenshmirtz's device?

Perry took the evil doctor's own remote and steered one of the -inators right through the wall.

What other way could you destroy his -inator?

Perry smashed one of Dr. Doofenshmirtz's -inators with a golf club.

What would you use to stop Dr. Doofenshmirtz's evil scheme?

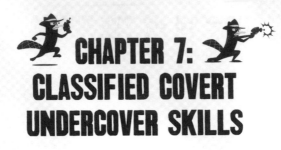

CHAPTER 7: CLASSIFIED COVERT UNDERCOVER SKILLS

Here are all the skills you need as an agent. These are the how-to details you've been waiting for, starting with one of the most important skills of all . . .

HOW TO MAKE A DRAMATIC ENTRANCE

Drop through a skylight.

Explode through a wall.

Slink in through the mail slot. (This one really only works if you're a snail.)

HOW TO DO THE RUMBA

In some rare, unlikely, bizarre circumstances, you may find yourself in a situation where you need to dance with your nemesis. Although we can't imagine why this would occur, it never hurts to be prepared.

- Face your nemesis.

- Put your right hand on the waist of your nemesis.

- Raise your left hand and hold the right hand of your nemesis.

- Move your left foot to the left, then your right foot.

- Move your left foot forward, then your right foot.

- Right foot back. Left foot back.

- Repeat.

IMPROVISING

An agent doesn't always have the latest equipment when he needs it, and he may find himself stuck in a situation where he has to improvise. With the right know-how, you can make a lock pick from a gum wrapper . . . or a laser beam from a paper clip and a ladybug. Here's how.

SCENARIO #1

You are locked in a room with nothing but a bat. You can't get through the door, but there is still a way out. **Swing the bat three times without hitting anything. Three strikes and you're out!**

SCENARIO #2

A villain traps you under a pile of rubble with his Trap-You-Under-a-Pile-of-Rubble-inator. You have nothing with you but a calendar. How can you survive until help arrives? **Simple. Open the calendar, and you can eat the *dates* and get water from the *spring*.**

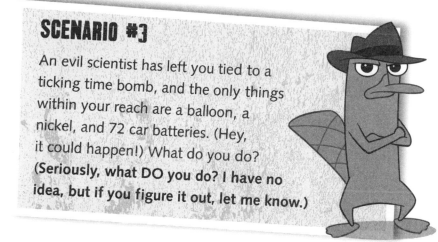

SCENARIO #3

An evil scientist has left you tied to a ticking time bomb, and the only things within your reach are a balloon, a nickel, and 72 car batteries. (Hey, it could happen!) What do you do? (Seriously, what DO you do? I have no idea, but if you figure it out, let me know.)

SECRET CODES AND YOU

While it's your job to uncover all the secrets of your nemesis, it's also important to keep your own secrets secret! That's where codes and ciphers come in.

CIPHERS

A cipher is a code that substitutes other symbols for the letters in the alphabet. Here's how *you* can do it. Write the alphabet down. Then write the alphabet again, just below the first one, but offset by one letter. So below A is B, below B is C, etc. When writing your coded message, look up the letter you want, but write down the letter beneath it. Using this code, "Perry" becomes "Qfssz."

STICK SCROLLS

Take a long, thin strip of paper and wrap it around a pencil or pen from one end to the other. Then write a secret message ACROSS the length of the paper. When you unwrap it, no one will understand a word of it.

INVISIBLE INK

Dip a toothpick in lemon juice and write a message on a piece of paper with the juice. When it dries, it will become invisible. Later on, have an adult hold the paper over a safe heat source (like a lightbulb) and watch the secret words appear.

UNDERWATER MANEUVERS

If you're semiaquatic like Agent P, operating underwater is a piece of cake. If not, you need to know how to fight underwater, give chase underwater, and survive underwater . . . but not necessarily in that order.

- Don't bump explosive mines. Don't hit, kick, or slap them either.

- Avoid creatures that will eat you. (This is good advice out of the water as well.)

- Remember to come up occasionally for air.

- Try to swim faster than your nemesis, either to catch up to him or get away from him. It works for both situations.

- Your movements will be slowed by the water, so hitting and kicking your opponent won't be as effective. If you have venomous spurs, now is the time to use them.

SURVIVING IN THE WILD

Staying alive in the comfort of your lair or host-family home is one thing, but do you know how to survive in the wilderness?

AVOID CAPTURE

1. If someone or something is after you, duck.

2. Blend in with your surroundings. Find some teal plants and stay there.

CREATE A SHELTER

1. Tie strong branches together for structure.

2. Weave large leaves over it for cover.

3. Add a whirlpool and flat-screen TV (optional).

FINDING SUSTENANCE

1. Forage for bugs, berries, and edible plants.

2. Catch and eat animals smaller than you. Eating animals larger than you can cause serious digestive problems.

CAN YOU DECIPHER DR. DOOFENSHMIRTZ'S BLUEPRINT?

Take a look at Dr. Doofenshmirtz's evil plans and see if you can unscramble the name of his latest -inator.

R
P
B
N
E
I
U
T
A
R
T
I
O
L
N

_____

(Answers on page 142)

CAN YOU ALSO DECODE WHAT THE EVIL SCIENTIST IS SAYING?

(Hint: Try reading the very first letter, and then just every other letter!)

CLUE ROSTER Y DONUT PRES ROREY AT THREE POLI AN TOY APRUNS

__ __ __ __ __ __ __

__ __ __ __ __ __

__ __ __ __ __ __!

(Answers on page 142)

CASE FILE #6028B

THE CASE OF THE BOUNCING BOOM JUICE

You can learn a great deal by studying the past exploits of successful agents.

In this case, Agent P was with his host family returning from a road-trip vacation when Major Monogram called. Apparently, Dr. Doofenshmirtz was nearby, driving a big rig overflowing with volatile boom juice, the explosive liquid he uses to make his -inators self-destruct!

Agent P leaped onto the eighteen-wheeler and attacked his nemesis, fighting both in the cab and atop the driverless vehicle as it barreled down the highway.

In the end, Perry sent the evil doctor's truck plummeting over the edge of a ravine to explode harmlessly below.

What can you learn from this? Persevere until the villain is defeated. And always wear your seat belt!

SECRET AGENT MEMORY TEST

Dr. Doofenshmirtz has clearly gone too far this time. Look at this scene for sixty seconds. Then turn the page and answer the questions to see how observant you are.

SECRET AGENT MEMORY TEST

Assuming you spent sixty seconds looking at the previous page, here are some serious questions to test your observational skills.

1) How many people can you see? _____ 8 _____

2) What is in the sky? _____ electricity _____

3) What is Dr. Doofenshmirtz wearing? _____ Under wear _____

_____

4) What is behind the three British dancers? _____ The _____
_____ inator _____

5) What is coming out of the big gray box? _____
_____ nothing _____

6) What is Carl holding? _____

_____

(Answers on page 142)

CHAPTER 8:
TOP SECRET FIGHTING TECHNIQUES

A good agent avoids conflict whenever possible, but sometimes a fight is unavoidable . . . especially when you're fighting evil. So you need to be prepared for the times when your only option is hand-to-hand combat. Or hand-to-webbed foot. Or hand-to-beaver tail. You get the idea.

DEFENSE

The best defense is a good offense, so why are you reading about defense?

OFFENSE

When a fight is inevitable, like if an evil genius is about to turn you into a tadpole or something, you should strike first. The element of surprise is on your side, and, honestly, who wants to be a tadpole. (Sorry, Agent T.)

STAY FOCUSED

Don't get distracted by talking robots, exploding -inators, or pitiful pleas for mercy from your nemesis. Stay on task until the job is done.

STAY GOOD

When in doubt, remain good. Good usually triumphs over evil.

FIGHTING STYLES

Look out! A squealing attacker springs at you from above, swinging his arms like a windmill! How do you respond? Here are the hand-to-hand combat styles that every good agent should know.

KARATE

Just like in the movies, use your hand as a weapon to subdue your opponent, chop through wood, and slice razor-thin vegetables.

BOXING

Feet apart. Head down. Hands up.
Knees bent. Mouth closed. Toes clenched.
Now put on your gloves and hit him!

KICKBOXING

Same as boxing, but the gloves go on your feet.

CAGE FIGHTING

Truth be told, it's pretty hard to fight when you are trapped in a cage. Our advice: escape from the cage, *then* fight.

AIKIDO

Redirect the force of your opponent, using the momentum of his attacks to flip, trip, and fling him. It not only deflects the attack, but it is really, really irritating to the attacker.

WRESTLING

Know these terms: Grapple. Drop. Pin. Tap out. (We don't have the definitions, but YOU definitely should.)

PROPER ENGLISH FISTICUFFS

Remove your jacket. Bow politely. Dance around your opponent as you trade witty verbal barbs. Grow fatigued and sit down for a cup of tea.

PLATY-KWON-DO

When the free world is at stake, an agent must do everything in his or her power to win the fight against evil . . . even if that means using the secret tricks of platy-kwon-do!

1) Point at your opponent's shoe. If you can talk, say, "Hey, your shoe's untied." When he looks down, hit him.

2) If you have a tail and your nemesis doesn't, use it! While he's busy keeping track of your legs and arms, swing that tail around for a surprise attack.

3) Fake left and then swing right. Works every time.

4) Gasp and point just over your opponent's shoulder. When he turns around, hit him.

5) Find his pressure points. Then put pressure on *them*.

6) Hand him a note. When he stops to read it, hit him.

CASE FILE #5297G
THE CASE OF THE DRUSELSTEINIAN DECAY

You can learn a great deal by studying the past exploits of successful agents.

When Perry burst in on his nemesis, he discovered a Druselstein-inator. It would transform everything it hit into a more old-fashioned, less-developed version of itself. By making Danville more like his backward home country of Druselstein, Dr. Doofenshmirtz would find it much easier to take over.

But Agent P made the daring move of actually leaping inside the -inator, battling his opponent in the tight quarters of the machine itself. When Dr. Doofenshmirtz was sufficiently pummeled, Agent P sent the -inator plummeting off the balcony.

What can you learn from this? Always think outside the box . . . but *inside* the -inator.

FINISH YOUR OWN COMIC

You tell us where this high-flyin' fight will lead.

THE PROS AND CONS OF FIGHTING IN SPACE

If you find yourself fighting in the inky blackness of outer space, here are some helpful tips.

OXYGEN

PRO: Much like on Earth, oxygen is key to living, and thus to fighting.

CON: Unfortunately, there isn't any oxygen up there.

GRAVITY

PRO: Without gravity, you can move in any direction, utilizing all three dimensions.

CON: Once you start heading in a direction, you can't stop. Better hold on to something!

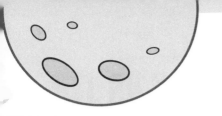

BACKUP

PRO: Every man, woman, and animal sent into space has a huge crew ready to back them up if anything goes wrong.

CON: That crew is thousands of miles away, down on Earth.

SPECTATORS

PRO: There are no people around to gawk at you or get in the way.

CON: Aliens may pull up, pop some popcorn, and watch the fight.

OBSTACLES

PRO: There aren't many obstacles to get in your way. That's why they call it *space*.

CON: When obstacles *do* come around, they are usually on fire and traveling thousands of miles an hour, so watch your step.

HOW WOULD *YOU* DO IT?

When Dr. Doofenshmirtz used his Metal-Unearth-inator to dig up metallic objects all over Danville, Perry the Platypus used various medieval objects to escape from his trap and fight with his nemesis.

That's how Perry solved this encounter with Doof. Now draw how you'd do it!

BATTLE TACTICS

Any agent will tell you that a fight varies dramatically depending on whom (or what) you are fighting. A technique that works well on a supervillain may not cut it when tussling with squirrels in your pants.

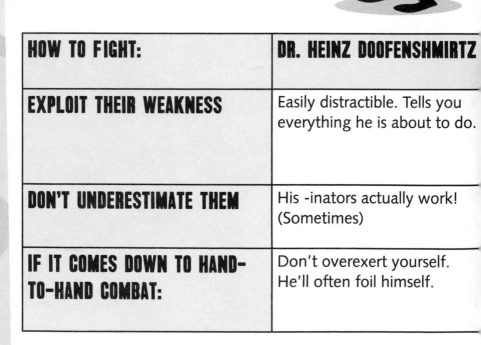

HOW TO FIGHT:	DR. HEINZ DOOFENSHMIRTZ
EXPLOIT THEIR WEAKNESS	Easily distractible. Tells you everything he is about to do.
DON'T UNDERESTIMATE THEM	His -inators actually work! (Sometimes)
IF IT COMES DOWN TO HAND-TO-HAND COMBAT:	Don't overexert yourself. He'll often foil himself.

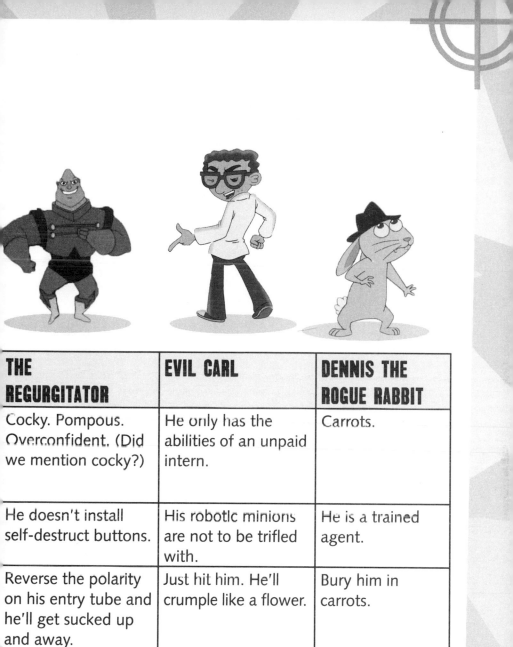

THE REGURGITATOR	EVIL CARL	DENNIS THE ROGUE RABBIT
Cocky. Pompous. Overconfident. (Did we mention cocky?)	He only has the abilities of an unpaid intern.	Carrots.
He doesn't install self-destruct buttons.	His robotic minions are not to be trifled with.	He is a trained agent.
Reverse the polarity on his entry tube and he'll get sucked up and away.	Just hit him. He'll crumple like a flower.	Bury him in carrots.

BATTLE TACTICS (CONTINUED)

You didn't think humans and rabbits were all you had to worry about, did you? What about fighting the inhuman monstrosities—cyborgs, androids, and robots?!

HOW TO FIGHT:	NORM	NORMBOTS
EXPLOIT THEIR WEAKNESS	He's not inherently evil, so ask him for some muffins and he'll run off to get some.	Their arms come right off! Use the detached arm to fire laser blasts right back at them.
DON'T UNDERESTIMATE THEM	Norm is the natural enemy of the platypus.	There are tons of them Literally *tons*.
IF IT COMES DOWN TO HAND-TO-HAND COMBAT:	He's powered by a squirrel in his heart, so just take the squirrel out.	Don't bother. Instead take out the tower controlling them.

PLATYBORG	THE FLYNN-FLETCHER BOTS
A platyborg has no weakness. It will not stop. It will not sleep. It will only destroy.	The Candace bot has a soft spot for the real Candace.
It has all of the abilities of a platypus *and* a cyborg.	Each robot has the ability to transform parts of its body into a formidable weapon.
A jolt of electricity should shake it up.	Grab the nearest screwdriver and disassemble them.

HOW TO FIGHT IN A BALL GOWN

What happens if you have to fight while wearing a fancy ball gown? Stranger things have happened. (I can't think of any right now, but they have.) So if you end up in a ball gown and have to fight, here are the top tips.

- If the gown is sequined, try to use the glittery reflection to distract your nemesis.

- Be careful not to trip on the train of your dress.

- If it's cold out and your gown is backless, you may want to take a shawl or a cover-up to keep warm.

YOU'LL HAVE TO *FIGHT* TO STOP LAUGHING!

Don't fight the feeling. You know you want to hear some more jokes. And these are sure to be knockouts. At least, that's what Major Monogram tells me.

What does Isabella say when she wants to borrow a stick of gum?

"Whatcha *chewin'*?"

What's a platypus's favorite fruit?

Gr-rr-rr-apefruit.

What did Phineas say when he saw his mom's broken lamp?

"Ferb, I know what we're gonna *glue* today!"

(MORE) PERRY TO THE RESCUE!

A FILL-IN-THE-BLANK ADVENTURE

Fill in the blanks to complete Perry's exciting mission below.

"Behold!" Dr. Doofenshmirtz cried, "my _____

NOUN

-inator!" The _____ scientist was actually *wearing* his

ADJECTIVE

latest -inator and it made him look _____!

ADJECTIVE

Perry knew that it would take all his _____ fighting

ADJECTIVE

skills to _____ Dr. Doofenshmirtz this time! Like

VERB

a _____ animal in the wild, Perry _____

ADJECTIVE   ADVERB

leaped at Doof, knocking over his large _____. Perry

NOUN

called on the ancient art of _____ -jujitsu and kicked

ANIMAL

a _____ at the evil doctor. Then, using the very

NOUN

_____ skills of ninja _____, Agent P

ADJECTIVE   PLURAL NOUN

pummeled his adversary like a _____ man. Despite

ADJECTIVE

his _____ -inator, Dr. Doofenshmirtz was no match for

NOUN

Perry's _____ attack. The evil scientist had to

ADJECTIVE

_____ to get away as Perry jumped to _____
VERB   VERB

Doof's -inator. As usual, Perry won, Doof lost, and goodness

and _____ were saved!
NOUN

THE END.

CHAPTER 9:
RESTRICTED AGENT EVALUATION

Now it's time to fill in the official O.W.C.A. Agent Application . . . *if* you think you're ready.

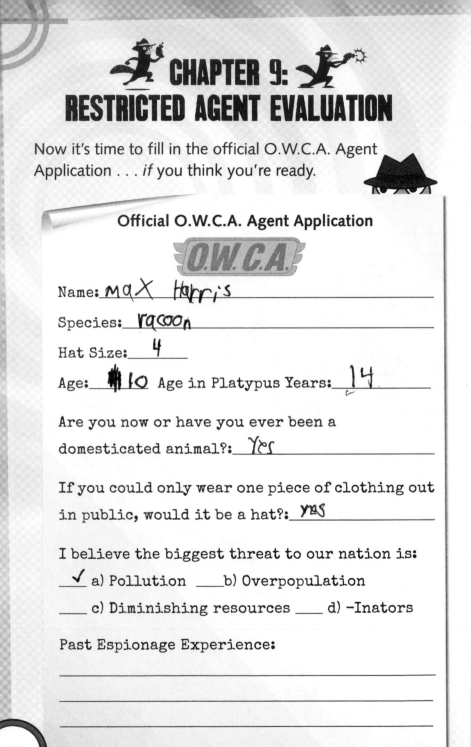

Official O.W.C.A. Agent Application

O.W.C.A.

Name: Max Harris

Species: racoon

Hat Size: 4

Age: ~~8~~ 10 Age in Platypus Years: 14

Are you now or have you ever been a domesticated animal?: Yes

If you could only wear one piece of clothing out in public, would it be a hat?: yas

I believe the biggest threat to our nation is:
___✓ a) Pollution ___b) Overpopulation
___ c) Diminishing resources ___ d) -Inators

Past Espionage Experience:

_____

_____

_____

_____

References (if they can be revealed):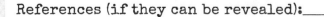_____

_____

_____

_____

_____

Areas of Expertise (Check all that apply):

__✓ Camouflage   __✗ Dental hygiene

__✓ Explosives   __✓ Grappling-hook maneuvers

__✓ Hand-to-hand combat   __✓ Hang gliding

__✓ Scheme-foiling   __ Semiaquaticness

__✓ Shorthand   __✓ Skydiving   __✗ Typing

Are you looking for a paid or unpaid position?:

____paid_____

Are you willing to sever all ties to the outside
world if hired?: __yes_____

How soon are you available to start?: __NOW____

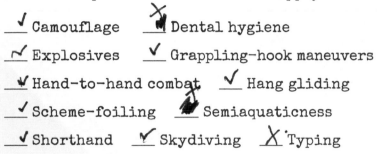

Please submit this form and wait for
contact. Do *not* try to contact us. We will
disavow all knowledge of your application.

TEST MISSION

This vital mission simulation will test your field skills in a virtual confrontation with Dr. Heinz Doofenshmirtz. Each decision you make leads you to a new box and another decision. Will you succeed, fail, or end up frozen in a block of gelatin?

START OVER

BOX 1
Travel to Doofenshmirtz Evil, Inc.

BOX 2
Knock at the door

BOX 3
Break down the door

BOX 4
Get trapped

BOX 5
Avoid trap

BOX 6
Get trapped in second trap

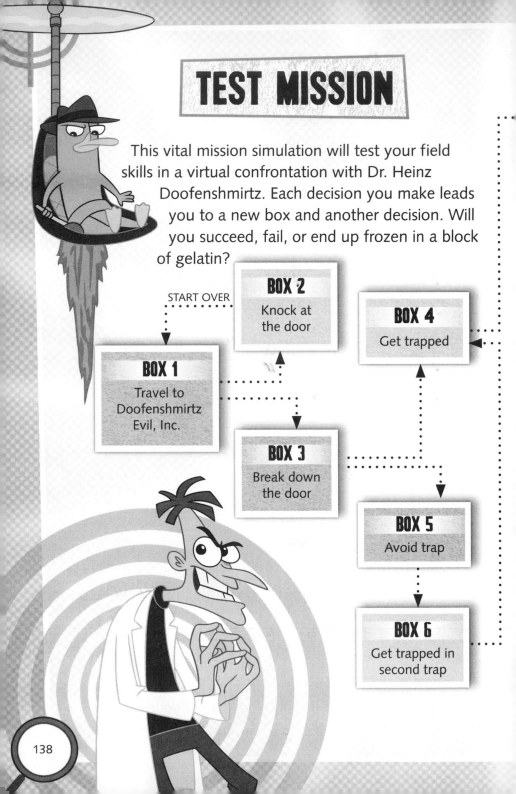

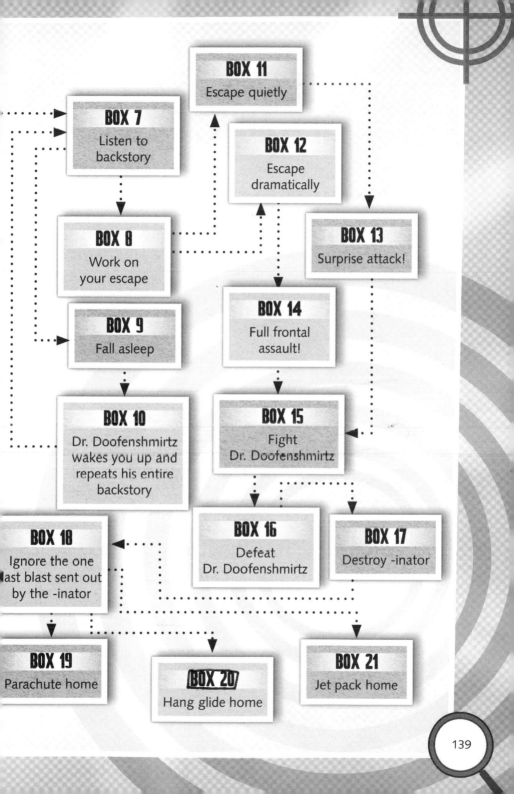

BOX 11
Escape quietly

BOX 7
Listen to backstory

BOX 12
Escape dramatically

BOX 8
Work on your escape

BOX 13
Surprise attack!

BOX 9
Fall asleep

BOX 14
Full frontal assault!

BOX 10
Dr. Doofenshmirtz wakes you up and repeats his entire backstory

BOX 15
Fight Dr. Doofenshmirtz

BOX 18
Ignore the one last blast sent out by the -inator

BOX 16
Defeat Dr. Doofenshmirtz

BOX 17
Destroy -inator

BOX 19
Parachute home

BOX 20
Hang glide home

BOX 21
Jet pack home

YOUR ULTIMATE SPY ADVENTURE

If the results of your tests are good, you'll be an agent in no time! You will be sent out on your first mission sooner than you think. But what kind of adventure awaits you? To see what's in store for you, circle one phrase from each column and write them in the blanks on the next page.

COLUMN A

Venice, Italy
A Hawaiian volcano
The Antarctic
My house
The moon
Downtown Danville
An alien zoo
A field of daisies
A planet made of trash

COLUMN B

Dr. Diminutive
Rodney
Professor Poofenplotz
The Regurgitator
Dennis the Rogue Rabbit
Mitch, enemy of Meap
The evil pirate Badbeard
An angry mailman
Lil' Suzy

COLUMN C

A dangerous sword fight
Cahoots with renegade janitors
A high-stakes game of cards
A fight with smelly cold cuts
A secret grotto full of snakes
A race for our lives
L.O.V.E.M.U.F.F.I.N.
A beautiful silk kimono
A martial-arts battle to the end

Write in your future assignments here:

For your first secret agent assignment, you'll travel to

___The Anarctic___ where you'll encounter
COLUMN A

___The regurgitator___ in _A dangerous sword fight_.
COLUMN B   COLUMN C

If you accomplish your introductory mission, then we'll

step things up by sending you to

___venice, italy___ to face
COLUMN A

down ___Mitch___
COLUMN B

in ___Martial arts___!
COLUMN C

141

CHAPTER 10:
COMPLETION: THE HIGHEST HONOR

If everything has gone according to plan, you have now completed the entire official O.W.C.A. training manual, otherwise known as "Agent P's Guide to Fighting Evil." Please take the time to check your work below.

PAGES 26-27: Agency Lingo Quiz: 1) B   2) B   3) C   4) C   5) C

PAGES 32-33: Agent P Trivia: 1) C   2) C   3) C   4) B   5) B

Bonus Question: It's *your* eye color!

PAGES 46-47: Agent Auditions: 1) No   2) No   3) Yes   4) No   5) Yes   6) No

PAGES 76-77: -Inator Names: 1) I   2) D   3) A   4) H   5) G   6) J   7) C   8) B
9) E   10) F

PAGES 86-87:

PAGE 89:

PAGE 112: Blueprint Code: Blueprint-inator

PAGE 113: Doof's Message: Curse You, Perry the Platypus!

PAGE 116: Memory Test: 1) Seven (Perry is not a person, but Carl, in the squirrel suit, is!)   2) Electrical arcs   3) Underwear, socks, and shoes. Ew! 4) Doof's -inator   5) Nothing!   6) The cage bars

SCORING:

Total up your correct answers. If you have more correct answers than incorrect, congratulations! You've passed! (We grade on a curve.)

ORGANIZATION WITHOUT A COOL ACRONYM

O.W.C.A.

This certificate of merit certifies that you have passed the rigorous training required to make you a

FULL-FLEDGED SECRET AGENT

With all the rights, privileges, and obligations that come with that position.

YOU ARE NOW READY TO FIGHT EVIL!

....